SOLOMON
and the TREES

Matt Biers-Ariel

Illustrated by

Esti Silverberg-Kiss

UAHC Press   ✲   New York

Library of Congress Cataloging-in-Publication Data

Biers-Ariel, Matt.
   Solomon and the trees / by Matt Biers-Ariel ; illustrated by Esti Silverberg-Kiss.
     p. cm.
   Summary: Tells the story of King Solomon and the origins of Tu B'Shevat, a holiday
that is celebrated by the planting of trees.
   ISBN 0-8074-0749-6 (alk. paper)
   [1. Tu bi-Shevat--Fiction. 2. Solomon, King of Israel--Fiction. 3. Jews--Fiction.] I.
Silverberg-Kiss, Esti, 1976- ill. II. Title.

PZ7.B4775 So 2000
[E]--dc21
                                     00-051145

To Yonah and Solomon,
my little princes
M B-A

❦

To Moshe and Daniella
E S-K

long time ago, in the Land of Israel, a young prince named Solomon lived next to a large forest. Solomon spent every spare moment in the forest because he preferred the company of the peaceful trees to his busy city life. Solomon made friends with the animals living there and learned to speak their language. They taught him secrets no human had ever learned, like how spiders keep from getting caught by their own webs and the reason bats sleep upside down. Solomon loved the forest, and the forest loved him.

The full moon of the Hebrew month Sh'vat was a magical time in the forest. Solomon would hike deep into the woods until he reached his favorite tree. Her color was creamy, golden brown, like butterscotch. Her wood was smooth as polished river stones. Taller than the other trees, she reigned over the forest, like a powerful queen protecting her subjects. Solomon gazed at this tree and knew that no work of man or woman could have ever created such beauty.

Each year at Sh'vat's full moon, Solomon sat at the base of this enormous tree. The birds that had flown south for the winter returned with stories of their adventures. Other animals crowded around and joined the cacophonous conversation.

Then came the magic. It always began with a slight stirring inside the tree, no louder than a flea's cough. Solomon raised his hand, and the animals ceased their chattering and listened. His ear on the trunk of the tree, Solomon heard what sounded like the starts and stops of water rumbling through an old, rusty pipe. Soon the rumbling gathered strength and became a rushing river flowing through the tree. After lying dormant all winter, the forest queen was drawing water up through her roots and sending it skyward to her thirsty limbs. This flowing water was the happiest music Solomon and his animal friends knew. It signaled a healthy new year not only for the tree, but for the entire forest. As long as the forest was healthy, Solomon knew his world would be well.

So it was, year after year, Prince Solomon witnessed the beginning of spring.

Out of the woods and back in the city, Solomon studied hard in school. With the knowledge he gained from both the forest and his books, the prince became known throughout the land as "Solomon, the Wise." Friends, family, and strangers came to him with their problems. Usually Solomon could discover a solution quickly. But for very difficult questions, Solomon would retreat into the woods and sit by the forest queen to think. The power of the tree helped him find the answer he was looking for.

The Land of Israel was ruled by Solomon's father, King David. After sitting on the throne for forty years, the time had come for him to pass the crown to one of his children. But to which one? David had many sons, each possessing his own greatness. One prince was the fiercest warrior in Israel. He would make a strong king who would protect his subjects. Another was known for his good nature. Everyone in the country loved him. He would be a popular king who could rally support for important causes.

King David closely examined each prince. He decided that of all the qualities a king must possess to rule well, wisdom was the most important. So before he died David anointed Solomon as king of Israel.

Solomon's first act as king was to build God's Temple in Jerusalem. God had not allowed David to build the Temple because of the many wars he had fought. God's Temple was to be a place of peace, so its builder needed to be a person of peace. Solomon was such a person. His life was dedicated to bringing peace to his fellow men and women, as well as to those in the animal and plant kingdoms. Even his name, "Solomon," stemmed from the Hebrew word for "peace."

To build the Temple, King Solomon hired the most skilled craftsmen in the land. The finest gold, the handsomest wood, the shiniest silver, the softest fabrics, and the most precious gems, all went into the construction of what many people thought of as the most beautiful building in the world.

At its completion, Solomon invited the entire country to the Temple's dedication. For the celebration, King Solomon's chief tailor surprised him with a royal robe of soft, purple velvet. The cuffs, collar, and hem were of black satin. Solomon's royal seal was embroidered over his heart in thread spun from gold. When the king slipped the robe on, it fit as though it were part of his body.

Not to be outdone, the king's chief jeweler presented him with a crown of pure gold set with sparkling diamonds, green emeralds, red rubies, and blue sapphires. The crown shone like a golden desert sunset. Never before had a flesh-and-blood king worn such a magnificent crown.

As Solomon walked up the Temple's steps wearing his robe and crown, the people murmured to each other that their king was the noblest man in the world.

When he reached the Temple gate, King Solomon was greeted by one last surprise: a throne carved by his chief carpenter. Each foot of the throne held the images of four faces: ox, lion, eagle, and man. Its four legs were crafted to look like palm trees. The ends of the curved armrests were shaped into pomegranates. The sides of the throne were engraved with grape leaves. The front of the throne's back held an image of a fig tree. Its back was covered with wheat and barley carvings. Perched on top of the throne was a dove holding an olive shoot, the symbol of peace.

Solomon gasped. Never had such beauty been created by the hand of a man or woman. King Solomon eased onto his throne and signaled for the dedication to begin. The people of Israel were happy. Not only was the Temple finally built, but they had a new king whom they knew would rule wisely.

As king, Solomon was forever called upon to make decisions, appear somewhere, or meet with advisors. Not a spare moment for himself and not a single visit to the forest. However, his heart ached for the trees, so when Sh'vat's full moon approached, the king left his crown by his bed, exchanged his royal robe for a backpack, and set off for the woods.

The moment Solomon reached the forest's edge, a strange feeling came over him. In the past, hundreds of birds would welcome him in excited voices, anxious to tell the latest news. Today not a single bird chirped hello, no lizards scurried through the leaves, not even a lone fly could be found buzzing through the air. Total silence greeted him.

"Ah, perhaps they've heard that I'm now king and have planned a surprise party," Solomon said to himself, smiling. As he walked on, the smile fell into a frown. Not only were the animals missing from the forest, but so were the trees. Where a beautiful oak once stood, Solomon found a stump. There was no sign of the cedar and cypress trees that intertwined about each other like husband and wife. In fact, all the large trees were missing. Only a few saplings remained here and there.

Solomon's heart raced as he ran through the devastated woods. Was the forest queen also gone? He crossed the stream that bordered the grove where she reigned. He held his breath and looked and saw an enormous stump where the giant tree once towered.

Solomon felt as though he had been hit in the chest. He gasped for air and stumbled to the stump. His companion and friend was dead, the forest destroyed. Pain and sadness filled Solomon's being. He placed his head in his hands. Tears streamed down his face.

After a long, hard cry, the heat of Solomon's anger dried his eyes.

"Those responsible will be punished, severely punished!" the king vowed.

But who did the deed? There was not a single creature to ask. Solomon searched and searched but could find no living soul. Finally, when he sat down to rest, he noticed a tiny black spider scurrying across his sandal.

"Spider," asked the king, "What happened? Tell me."

"Woodcutters chopped the trees," the spider yelled at the top of its voice. "Then the animals left."

"Woodcutters! Which direction did they go?"

The spider pointed a leg to the northwest.

After thanking the spider, the king walked three days until he spied smoke from a wood mill. Solomon barged into the mill. When the three woodsmen saw their king glowering in the doorway, fear grabbed them and they fell on their faces.

Solomon lifted the nearest man off the floor and shook him like a dirty carpet. "Why did you cut down the forest? Are you mad?"

Shock left the poor man speechless.

"Speak!" commanded the king as he dropped the woodsman on the floor. The terrified man looked to his friends. They encouraged with their eyes.

"Your Highness," he sputtered, "we cut the trees for . . . for . . . you."

"For me!" Solomon roared, his face blazing red. "I commanded no such thing!"

In a whisper as soft as a downy feather, the woodsman replied, "For the . . . the Temple."

"The Temple," Solomon repeated. A faraway look glazed over his eyes. Like a chameleon, the color of his face instantly changed from bright red to sickly green. His legs no longer able to support him, Solomon slid down the wall and sat crumpled up on the floor.

"Your throne, too," added a second woodsman. "The chief carpenter asked us to bring him the finest wood for your throne. We searched the entire forest until we found the tallest and most beautiful tree. The color of its wood was golden brown, and its bark was smooth as if it had been sanded with the finest sandpaper."

"The forest queen," murmured Solomon.

"Your Majesty?"

"Nothing," Solomon replied. He picked himself up and started out the door.

"Your Majesty?" the confused men called after him.

The king dismissed them with a wave of his hand.

Solomon walked back to the forest and thought and thought and thought some more.

"True, the trees went to a noble cause," Solomon concluded. "Yet, it's also true that because of me the forest is gone;therefore, it is upon me to bring it back."

Solomon arose early next morning and combed through the forest floor for seeds and cones dropped by the felled trees. He returned to his palace, germinated the seeds, and tended the young plants. One year later at Sh'vat's full moon, King Solomon returned to the forest to plant a basket of seedlings. Year after year he returned to the forest on the first day of spring to plant trees. After five years the birds began to come back. After twenty years a young forest emerged. After forty years an offspring of the forest queen towered over a healthy forest.

King Solomon was satisfied. His work was completed. By now Solomon was an old man. His time as king was also finished. He stepped down from the throne, and within the year he died.

Year after year during the reign of King Solomon, the people of Israel had watched their beloved king hike into the forest to plant seedlings. After his death the people continued planting, thus insuring that their forests would live forever.

A holiday was declared to commemorate this day of tree planting. Even to this day the people Israel go out at the full moon of Sh'vat, that is, the fifteenth day of Sh'vat, known as Tu BiSh'vat in Hebrew, to plant trees.

Sources

🌿 *Solomon and the Trees* is a modern midrash. A midrash is a story that is based on a story or a passage from the Bible. Many midrashim have been written about the wisdom of King Solomon. The Bible makes the following claim:

> He was wiser than all men. . . . His fame spread throughout all the surrounding nations.
>
> *1 Kings 5:11*

King Solomon's wisdom was not limited to the human realm, but also encompassed the natural world, including the ability to speak the language of animals. This attribute stems from the biblical verse 1 Kings 5:13:

> He spoke about trees, from the cedar in Lebanon to the hyssop that grows out of the wall. He spoke about the beasts, the birds, creeping things, and fishes.

Seven species of plants are held sacred in the Land of Israel based on the biblical verse Deuteronomy 8:8. These plants are those that are carved into the king's throne in *Solomon and the Trees*. Mention is made in *Solomon and the Trees* of a cedar tree and a cypress tree that intertwined about each other as husband and wife. At one time it was a common Jewish practice to plant a cedar at the birth of a son or a cypress at the birth of a daughter. When the child was ready for marriage, limbs from the tree are used for huppa poles.

While the Bible does not make mention of the deforestation in the ancient Middle East, it is believed that the ancient Middle East was a more forested environment than it is today. While Solomon actually used wood from Lebanon to build both the Temple and his sumptuous palace, the quantity of wood used in just these two building projects was enormous and likely strained forest resources.

Tu BiSh'vat

Tu BiSh'vat, literally the fifteenth day of the month of Sh'vat, is the New Year for the trees as designated in the Mishnah. While Tu BiSh'vat began as the day when taxes were levied on fruit trees, it has evolved into what it is today—a holiday celebrating trees and nature.

In the medieval Ashkenazi communities of Europe, a custom arose of eating fifteen kinds of fruit on Tu BiSh'vat. Special attention was placed on eating carob as well as the fruit from the seven sacred plant species mentioned in Deuteronomy.

In the 1500s, the Jewish mystics of Tzfat, a mountainous town in the Galilee, created a Tu BiSh'vat seder patterned after the Passover seder. This seder was a mystical journey into the four kabalistic worlds of Creation. Every year since the early 1980s more and more people and communities have been holding Tu BiSh'vat seders in order to renew their connections to the natural world of God's Creation.

Yet, the most widely practiced Tu BiSh'vat custom is tree planting, with a special emphasis on planting in Israel. Biologically speaking, Tu BiSh'vat is an appropriate time to plant in Israel, since the holiday falls in the winter, when the majority of trees lie dormant.

Whether it is celebrated by eating fifteen varieties of fruit, holding a seder, or planting trees, Tu BiSh'vat has become the "Jewish Earth Day."